Rudy

A Big Horse with
a Big Heart

by
Diane Robbins Jones

Illustrated by
Karen Busch Holman

Printed by King Printing, Lowell, Massachusetts.

Cover and interior illustrations and book layout design by Karen Busch Holman.

Disclaimer

This book is entirely created by the author's interpretation and recollection of past events. Some names and characteristics have been changed, events altered, and dialogue recreated. The views, thoughts, and opinions expressed herein belong solely to the author, and are not necessarily the views of any other individual, group, or organization. The author's views thereby, do not reflect the publisher's views. Hwin and Little Bear Press hereby disclaims any responsilbility for them.

Hwin&LittleBearPress

hwinandlittlebearpress.com

TABLE OF CONTENTS

ACKNOWLEDGEMENTS

My undying gratitude and appreciation to Rudy for making my dream come true and enriching my life in unimaginable ways. I believe we were meant to come together. I treasure every minute I am in your magnificent presence.

To Erik Kowalski, for encouraging me to pursue my lifelong dream, and tolerating more horse conversation than a non-horse person should endure.

To my mother, who entertains my endless "Rudy" stories with never-ending excitement and enthusiasm. I love that I can share this dream and joy with you, and how you call him your "Grand-horse."

A huge thanks to Allison Smith, Rudy's angel, for seeing Rudy for who he truly is, and helping me see him in the same way. There are no words to express my gratitude for all your support in the forms of time, wisdom, and love. Thank you for introducing me to your "dream team" of horse experts, giving Rudy and me the best chance of succeeding. Without you, we wouldn't be where we are today, and this book may not have become a reality.

To my niece Cecelia Robbins, who loves horses as much as me, and never tires of my "Rudy" stories or pictures. It is magic to spend time together with you and Rudy. I love how you approach him without fear, but a perfectly open heart. He in turn responds to you with gentleness and curiosity.

To Howard Jacobs, for encouraging me to write, and more importantly, for being a "safe" outlet to share my writing. You've helped me find the confidence to put myself out there, and for that I'm extremely grateful. Thank you for your willingness to make something that's important to me important to you.

To Irene Tomkinson, a debt of gratitude to you for your encouragement, love, and support. I am finding my voice!

Thank you, Deanna Kravetz, for being a wonderful trainer. Your support and encouragement to Rudy and me are appreciated more than you know. I love your sensitive, intuitive ways. I appreciate the reminders to be kind to myself.

To Peyton Stading, for being the first child I shared this book with in its entirety. Your interest in Rudy and the writing process has been inspirational.

My "dream team" knows who they are—Rudy and I thank you from the bottom of our hearts. We are deeply grateful for your knowledge, compassion, and guidance. We are blessed to have you in our lives.

A special thank you to my family and friends for your support on this uncharted journey.

FORWARD

Never give up on your dreams! This book is proof you can make them come true if you hold them in your mind and heart.

I've always had a passion and love for animals. As a child, I begged my Mom for kittens, insisted we go down the street whenever the local farmer had a calf being born, and obsessed over horses. When I was in elementary school, a girl in my neighborhood had a pony, and this ignited a desire within me to have my own horse.

I began the quest to find the "right" horse, which meant a cheap one. I knew my family didn't have enough money, nevertheless, I was convinced that if I found an inexpensive horse somehow it would be possible.

Week after week I scoured the local papers for horses for sale. Many weeks I found a candidate and would excitedly show my Mom the ad as I spent several minutes exuberantly making my case for why this was the "right" horse. Time after time, she'd gently explain why neither of us could buy a horse. We didn't have the money, land, barn, time, or knowledge to own a horse. Disappointed, I'd take the paper into my bedroom and stare at the ads, refusing to believe it wasn't possible.

I never did get a horse as a kid, a teenager, or once I was out on my own as an adult but I never gave up on the dream. I'd tell people "I'll have a horse someday, when the timing is right."

In 2015, at age 50, the timing was right. I had moved from Massachusetts to Portsmouth, New Hampshire. I had been thinking of taking horseback riding lessons for a few years, but my career had kept me too busy.

In Portsmouth, there was a stable a mile from my house. I thought to myself, "If I can't make this work, it will never work." I made a New Year's resolution to start riding lessons. Several days into January, I had my first lesson.

Over the next few months, I became friendly with the stable owner as well as some of the workers. To be around the horses more, I started helping with chores at the barn. I was clocking more equine time than I had in years. I was pleased with myself for finally making horses a priority in my life when I learned Rudy's owner wanted to sell him.

I had already noticed Rudy—something about him intrigued me. For starters, he was a big "red" horse, but it was more than just his physical appearance calling to me. I felt as though he was misunderstood. I felt he needed someone to commit to him and give him a chance to shine.

I had conversations with the stable owner, Rudy's owner, and a few other people before I decided to start working with him. After a month, I was pleased with the progress we were making. I asked his owner if I could lease him for a few more months before making the decision to buy him. She agreed.

I knew nothing about owning a horse, much less a huge Thoroughbred who hadn't been worked with any consistency over the past few years. The stable owner, as well as one of the boarders at the barn, Allison Smith, helped me navigate the new, sometimes overwhelming, but often exciting world of horse training.

Rudy and I continued to make progress in our work together and after several months passed I was encouraged enough to take the plunge—I bought him for $1. This story chronicles the beginning of our journey together—told by Rudy, for it is my belief he can tell it best.

Disclaimer

This book is entirely created by the author's interpretation and recollection of past events. Some names and characteristics have been changed, events altered, and dialogue recreated. The views, thoughts, and opinions expressed herein belong solely to the author, and are not necessarily the views of any other individual, group, or organization. The author's views thereby, do not reflect the publisher's views. Hwin and Little Bear Press hereby disclaims any responsilbility for them.

New York: City Kid

Hi, my name is Rudy, well that's my name today, but let me start by telling you a little bit about me and where it all began. I was born at a barn near the Saratoga Race Course in New York.

Even though Saratoga is far from New York City, I was given the name "City Kid"—my registered Thoroughbred name. My owners bred me with the hope I'd be a great race horse and win many races. As a colt, I trained to run as fast as I could on the track. It was tough work, and even though I tried hard, my trainers gave up on me because I wasn't fast enough.

You would think I'd be a great race horse for I am very tall (17.1 hands) with long muscular legs, and a strong chest. The problem? I'm easy going. I didn't want to run fast every time we practiced. Sometimes I ran hard, other times I didn't. Maybe that's why I was never entered in one race?

When my owners stopped trying to make me into a race horse, no one paid much attention to me. I spent most days in a paddock. I enjoyed munching on sweet grass, but I was lonely.

I eventually moved to a new barn. A woman started working with me in a new way. She rode me frequently, and called me "Rudy." We practiced fancy ways of moving my feet, a discipline she called "dressage."

Dressage is done in an arena, not on a race track. It felt good to work again and even better to have someone pay attention to me. I thought I was doing a good job, but one day I was loaded into a trailer. I was surprised to see I was back at the old barn. As it turned out, I wasn't good at dressage, or at racing.

For the next few years, I spent my time alone in a stall or paddock. My owner was busy working with other horses at the stable, but on occasion she'd come see me. I could tell she liked me, but was too busy to spend time with me.

I became bored and depressed. I lost weight and muscle because I didn't always get enough food to eat. The people at the barn must have thought I didn't need as much since I wasn't working. I often hung my head down searching for small nibbles of grass as I wondered, what's wrong with me?

CHAPTER TWO

Big Move

One cold December day, I was loaded into the trailer. This was definitely not one of my favorite things to do. Horses are prey animals so we're most comfortable when all paths of escape are available. In the trailer I was trapped, and this made me so scared. And when it moved, I struggled to keep my balance.

We left New York early in the morning and traveled most of the day. I was weary when we arrived in Portsmouth, New Hampshire. My owner opened the trailer door and slowly backed me out.

While I was relieved to be outside, I didn't recognize anything around me. This put me on edge. I snorted when something rustled in the wind and I scanned the area for danger. People surrounded me, but I didn't know any of them.

The first person to approach me was a girl. She seemed excited and immediately began touching me. I shifted my weight nervously as I looked over my shoulder and flared my nostrils to breathe in her scent. It seemed the people were giving me a little time to adjust to the new environment. They stood nearby and chatted as I inquisitively looked around.

Then, without warning, something tugged on my blanket. I instinctively kicked out with my hind foot, connecting with whatever had touched me. I heard a loud wail, "OUCH!" yelled the barn worker. There was a commotion as people rushed to her. I heard one of them say, "I think your wrist is broken!" I didn't mean to hurt anyone. I was already afraid and the sudden touch near my rump made me think I was being attacked.

The injured person, as well as a couple other people, hurried away. Everyone seemed tense and this made me even more nervous. My owner led me into the barn. My new stall had hay on the floor and a bucket of water hanging from the wall. I lowered my head and took a bite of hay, happy to feel a bit more comfortable. I looked up just as my owner walked out of the barn. The girl who stroked my neck earlier stood in the doorway. Before she left for the night, she came over and petted my neck again.

It was obvious I'd gotten off to a rough start at my new home, but I was hopeful things would get better and at first, they were, I had more food and I slowly began to gain weight. I was no longer bored or lonely because during the day I was turned out in a paddock with other horses.

CHAPTER THREE

Miscommunications

My new owner, the young girl who greeted me the day I arrived, was named Sophie. She was full of excitement, and I felt her love for me right away!

At first, she came to the barn almost every day. She bought me many new things, a fancy leather halter with my name on it, saddle pads in all the colors of the rainbow, a new saddle, blankets, and much more. I felt beautiful when she put these things on me. We often worked in the riding arena where I trotted or cantered around holding my head high to show off my strength and agility.

Sophie and I did many fun things in the first few months together. Besides working in the arena, we rode in the fields below the barn. She also took me on the trails. In those moments, I thought things couldn't be better.

Things were always changing though. Sophie had lots of ideas of things she wanted to try with me. I liked some of her ideas, but others frightened me. If she groomed me, gave me treats, or let me eat the lush, green grass in the field, I was happy. I usually didn't mind when we rode in the arena or the field, but often I got scared when we rode on the trails.

I communicated my fear the only way I knew how, through body language. The problem is most people don't understand this language. Humans make sounds with their mouths. I don't understand most of the sounds and this leads to many misunderstandings. Just ask Sophie.

Many things contributed to my fear and resistance. I hadn't worked with people in a long time. I was used to being on my own, which meant I was used to just being a horse. Horses have a long history of successfully working with humans but we'd prefer to be with a herd of other horses roaming free and nibbling on forage day in and day out.

My training in New York didn't include being ridden in the woods so this was all new to me. And, as a Thoroughbred, I can be quick to react, or spook. I was ten years old, an age many would expect I'd be a "finished" horse, comfortable in his surroundings and his people. In reality, I was quite "green" or inexperienced.

One time, Sophie and I came out of the woods and I wanted to get back to the safety of the barn as fast as possible. I started trotting, then broke into a canter, followed by a gallop.

Sophie pulled back on the reins hard. As we sped along, the ground was quickly closing in on a ditch filled with water. I did what came naturally to me, I jumped. As my hooves hit the ground, I felt a sudden lightness on my back and heard a "thud." Oh no, Sophie fell off! I was surprised, but too afraid to stop.

I stopped running only as my chest collided with the fence of a paddock with a loud "CLANK"! I stood there huffing and puffing as I tried to catch my breath. I was relieved to be back, but Sophie wasn't pleased.

Several minutes passed before she caught up with me. She grabbed the reins with a sharp tug and pulled me with her. She didn't talk to me or pat me as we walked to the barn. Once in the barn, she slid off the saddle and bridle and led me back to the paddock. The gate closed with a sharp "clink" as she turned and walked up the hill.

There was another time I became frightened, when we worked in the arena. She took off the lead rope and slapped a whip on the ground near me. The "crack, crack, crack" startled me. I jumped sideways and took off running. I ran in circles as she slapped the rope on the ground near me. My heart pounded, my body tensed, and my eyes grew wide with fear. I didn't understand what she wanted me to do.

I scaled a couple of jumps in my panic. Eventually, I realized she was standing still in the middle of ring. Exhausted, I stopped. I was still on high alert when she came over to me. I shied away when her hand reached up to pat my neck. She said "good boy," and clipped the rope onto my halter. As we walked out of the arena I thought, is that really what she wanted me to do? It was so scary!

I tried to do the things Sophie asked of me, but I also had to let her know how I felt. I liked her, but sometimes I didn't feel safe with her. Past events taught me not to fully trust her. Because I felt this way I bucked, ran, or tossed my head when I got scared. Sophie fell off me several times, and I could feel her fear growing with each fall.

Her body was tense when she rode me. She held tightly onto the reins. I wondered why she was afraid. If she was, then perhaps I should be afraid too. I reacted to the smallest sounds. A snap of a twig or the rustle of leaves made me flinch, jump, or bolt. She came to see me less as the days passed. I didn't think much about this at first, but when the days turned into weeks I wondered if she had given up on me.

I missed her attention. Once again, I had no one to rely on but myself. I expressed my frustration by kicking the stall walls, sometimes breaking the boards. When the barn workers handled me, I crowded them or dragged them to the grass so I could graze. If they put me on the cross ties in the barn I often expressed my anxiety by shaking my head up and down over and over. It seemed I was on the fast track to becoming a "problem" horse.

CHAPTER FOUR

Free and Famous

That first winter in New Hampshire, it snowed a lot! There is nothing like fresh fallen snow to make horses frisky. We held our heads high, flared our nostrils as we breathed in the cold, crisp air while our manes and tails blew in the wind. Full of energy, we chased each other around bucking and rearing. This helped us blow off steam as well as keep warm.

The snow piled up in the paddocks and before long the ground was higher and the fences lower. The perfect recipe for adventure! One March morning I lifted up my front leg and stepped over the fence. One leg, two legs, three legs, four legs, I was free! Charm and Jaunty, the other two horses in the paddock decided to step over too. Maybe we could find some yummy grass instead of all of this snow!

I led the way as we walked down the long dirt driveway. I got to the end of the driveway and turned right onto a road. We sauntered casually down the street as cars pulled off to the side to let us pass. We must have been quite a sight!

All three of us had chestnut hair, a reddish-brown color, white markings on our face, and we were wearing our winter blankets. Blankets are like jackets for horses. They buckle around our bellies and help keep us warm on cold days. I was wearing my red blanket, Charm was in his grey and blue blanket, and Jaunty was in her purple and blue blanket. We were a colorful bunch of lookalike horses on the loose.

We became aware something was following us as we paraded down the road in single file. It was the police! They drove behind us slowly. Soon we heard familiar voices, the owner of the stable and other barn workers. Lead ropes in hand they walked up to us, clipped the ropes on to our halters, turned us around, and started walking us back to the barn.

I must admit I put up a fuss when I was asked to step onto the sidewalk. Meanwhile, traffic stood still. People sat in their cars with heads craned as they looked out their windows at us. When we got back to the barn, we were put in our stalls while the barn workers cleared the snow out of the paddocks. They seemed upset, which we didn't understand. All we wanted to do was go exploring.

The next day, I heard the barn workers talking about a story in the local newspaper titled, "Loose horses prompt police call, traffic snarl in Portsmouth."[i] The story was accompanied by three pictures of us walking down the street. We were famous!

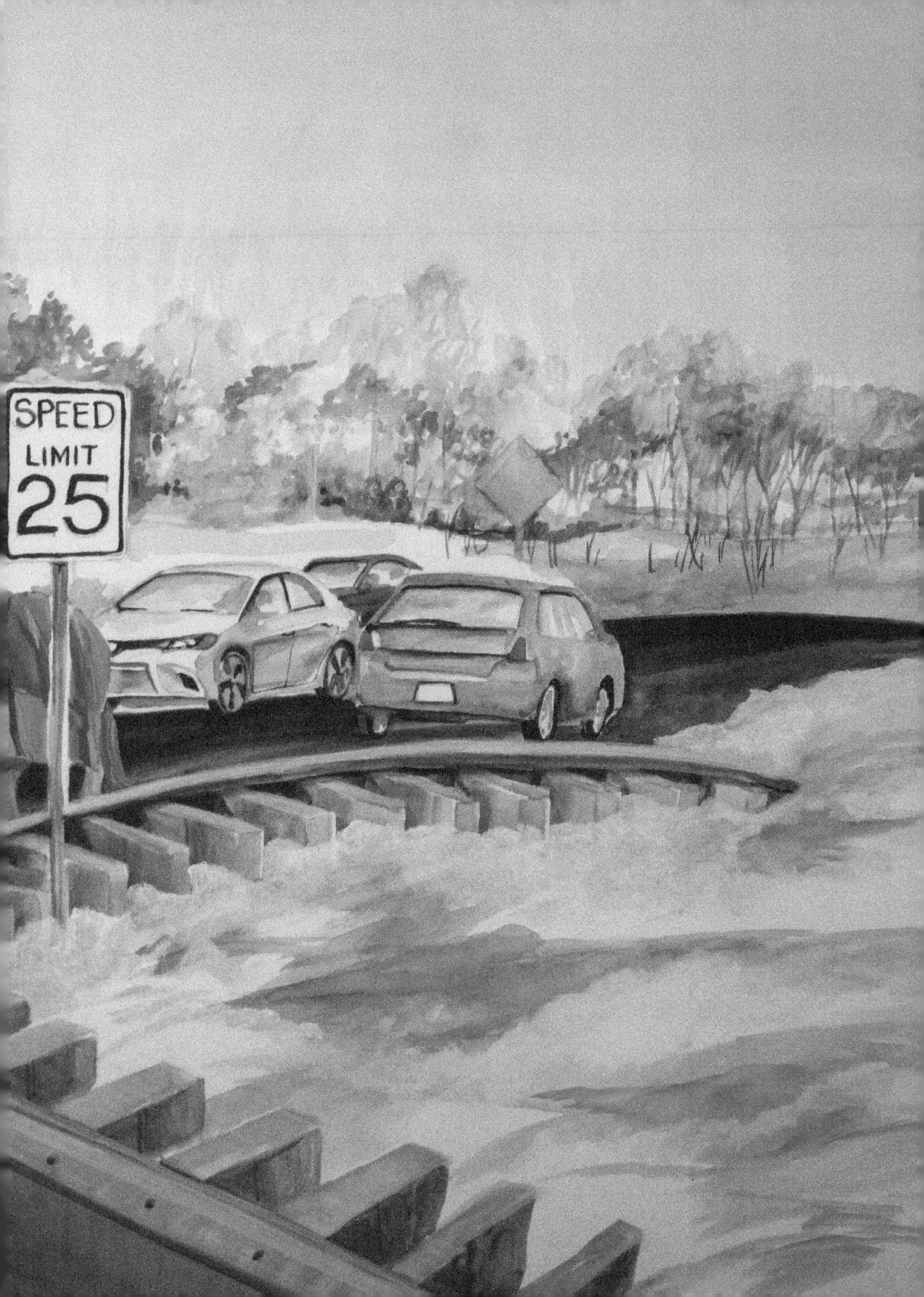
SPEED
LIMIT
25

CHAPTER FIVE

My Best Friend Shadow

Let me introduce you to Shadow. Who is Shadow? Shadow was the best friend anyone could ever want. I shared a paddock with him since my escape with Charm and Jaunty. When we weren't in the paddock, we were in separate stalls but our stalls were side by side.

This provided us with easy access to each other when the workers left our doors open. We'd stick our heads out to sniff each other or playfully nip at each other's face. Nips aren't like bites—they don't hurt or pull off hair or skin. They are a fun gesture between buddies.

My favorite thing about Shadow—he always wanted to play so we rough housed a lot! It usually started with him giving me small nips on my face or neck. Sometimes it took a while to get me going, but Shadow didn't give up easily. He kept nipping at me or rearing up on his hind legs to encourage me to play. His persistence usually paid off, and it was "game on!"

In response, I would rear up towering above him and as I came down I would swing my head in his direction, mouth open to deliver a playful nip. Shadow would anticipate my move and dart away. He would spin around and lunge at my rump, intentionally missing it.

Around and around we would go until we got tired. When we stopped we would stand close to each other as we caught our breath. We'd let out big sighs, satisfied with our antics.

Shadow was tough, really tough, even though he was much smaller than me. He was a Rocky Mountain horse. He had thick, dark brown hair, and a wavy blond mane that flew up when he ran. Before he moved to New Hampshire, Shadow lived in Colorado and was a search and rescue horse.

As a search and rescue horse, Shadow would take riders into the mountains to look for lost or injured people. He was good at this job because Rocky Mountain horses are confident and skilled at navigating steep, heavily forested mountains. True to his breed, Shadow rarely became scared or bothered.

In fact, he didn't even mind the flies while I did. I still find them unbearable. I constantly stomp my feet, swish my tail, and spin my head around to chomp them, but Shadow would eat or doze in the sun paying no attention to the pests. I can't understand how this is possible. In my mind, one fly is one fly too many!

I loved Shadow because he always wanted to be with me. Often he would stand next to me, in my shadow. Could this be how he got his name? When I walked to the other side of the paddock, he followed a step or two behind me but close enough for me to know he was there. I felt comforted having my friend close by. If Shadow wasn't in the paddock with me, he'd whinny loudly to me and I whinnied back to let him know I was okay. I hope you now understand why he was my best friend.

CHAPTER SIX

My New Person

I began to notice a new person at the barn in the spring. I heard people call her Diane. She helped the barn workers with some chores. There always seemed to be plenty of chores.

The workers start their day early. The first thing they do is give each horse a flake of hay. A flake is a section of a square bale of hay, the way it naturally divides. I listened to a lot of talk at the barn and learned bales of hay are measured in weight and in flakes. While the horses munch on their hay, the farm hands put more hay in the paddocks in preparation for us being turned out. They also check the water troughs to make sure they are full.

After the paddocks are prepped, the staff pours the grain into our buckets. All the horses have a bucket with their name on it. Each horse gets a different type and amount of grain. Some horses get supplements.

The quantity and formula of grain a horse gets depends on its size, age, workload, and breed. Generally, bigger horses get more grain; smaller horses get less. Younger horses usually get less and older horses get more. It's important there are no mix ups with the grain buckets.

A new type of grain or supplement can upset a horse's stomach. An upset stomach in a horse is called "colic." A severe case of colic can make the horse very sick and even result in death because horses can't throw up like humans can when they don't feel good.[ii] For this reason, workers must pay careful attention to ensure the correct buckets are given to the right horses.

Once we finish breakfast, the staff prepares us for turnout. Some horses get protective boots, fly masks, bug spray, or blankets in the winter. Each horse also gets a halter and a lead rope. The workers lead us to the paddocks and put us out with our herd group. This is my favorite part of the day because I get to play with Shadow.

Now, the hard work starts for the staff. They clean each stall removing the urine and manure with a stall fork, sifting and separating the dirty bedding from the clean. A stall fork is similar to a fork you eat with but much bigger. After removing the dirty bedding, they add clean bedding for the coming night. Bedding is usually wood shavings, saw dust, or straw.

While I'm outside I see, hear, and smell lots of things. I see and hear the workers, and sometimes Diane, doing chores. I hear water coming out of the hose and splashing into buckets as they get filled. I notice the squeak of the wheels on the wheelbarrows as they are pushed and then emptied.

If I listen closely, I can hear the grain being prepared for our dinner. Animals called dogs run around playing in the field. Sometimes people call to them loudly to get them to come back to the barn. After lunch riders may come to work their horses.

Small birds dart around chipping. Occasionally, bigger birds with red tails soar over the field screeching. Most of the time, I ignore all this activity. I meander around with my nose close to the ground sniffing for the sweetest bites of grass and other yummy plants like clover.

It's usually mid-day by the time the stalls are ready. This means it's lunch time. The staff brings more hay to the paddocks. They spread it around into piles to help prevent us from fighting.

Horses have to get fed hay throughout the day to keep them from getting stomach ulcers since they evolved from grazing all day in the wild. I love lunch and claim a big pile for myself. We need lots of water, too, and our water troughs are again checked.

Before sundown, the workers bring us in and put us in our stalls for the night. Our dinner hay is already in our stalls and our water buckets are full. They give us a short time to munch on our hay before they pour our grain into our buckets, close and lock the stall doors for the night. Rain or shine, day in-day out, this is the routine of the barn.

I first noticed Diane at the barn in the evenings. She helped the staff bring us in and feed us. Weeks passed and she kept coming to the stable. Sometimes she helped with chores. Other times she took horses out for rides. One of the horses she took out was Shadow. I often caught her looking at me when she came to get him. I'd stare back at her for a few seconds with my big brown eyes before going back to grazing.

Several times she stood at the fence looking at me as if to beckon me. One time my curiosity got the best of me. I strolled over, flared my nostrils, and breathed in her scent. I reached my head over the fence and felt her hand gently stroke the hair on my neck.

Days later, she was there again standing at the gate to my paddock. I figured she was coming to get Shadow, but then I noticed she was looking at me. She walked toward me slowly and stopped near my shoulder. Oddly, she didn't try to touch me. She stood next to me and I could hear her breathing slowly.

I turned my head toward her and sniffed. Something was different. I didn't feel as nervous as I did with other people. She seemed to know I was afraid sometimes. She made sounds with her mouth and even though I didn't know what they meant, they made me feel calm. They sounded like "goooood boy, goooood boy."

Diane held out my halter. I lowered my head and slid my nose in as she pulled it over my ears and clipped the strap under my chin. Next, she opened the gate. I wasn't sure what we were doing so I hesitated. She gently encouraged me to come. Haltingly, I stepped out of the paddock and followed her up the hill.

Once we got inside the barn, she clipped the cross ties to my halter and began to carefully groom me. Brushing a horse loosens dirt and debris in our hair and helps prevent sores from developing on our back when tack is put on. It also provides the person with an opportunity to check us over for any injuries or health problems such as cuts or skin infections.

After brushing the horse, it's important to pick the horses hooves. Using a tool with a blunt metal point and a brush each hoof is checked and cleaned of dirt and pebbles. A small rock lodged in my foot can cause a painful hoof bruise and I could go lame.

Grooming is also a way for humans to create a bond with the horse. As Diane groomed me, I felt the bristles of the brush glide over my hair. No one had brushed me since Sophie stopped coming and I had tons of itchy spots. She took her time and got every last one. I tried to let her know how much I liked this by wiggling my lips, stretching my jaw, and yawning.

Horses don't yawn when they are tired. Horses yawn when they are feeling less anxious. Yawning is called a "release." I frequently turned my head around to look at her as she worked. When she finished, she took me off the cross ties and walked me out of the barn toward the arena.

She asked me to walk next to her without tugging on the rope as we went around. I wasn't allowed to go too fast or too slow. She told me to back up and to move over to give her more space. I had done these things before, but it had been a while. It took me a little time to understand what she wanted. Even though I was rusty, I thought I did a pretty good job. As we strolled out of the arena Diane patted my neck and said, "Goooood boy, goooood boy." I sighed, relieved to be heading back to the barn.

CHAPTER SEVEN

My Friend Diane and I Work Together

Diane continued coming to the barn. We worked alone or with the barn's owner. Every session began with grooming. She was always gentle and took care to make me look my best.

While this was my favorite part of our time together, there was one exception—I didn't like having my feet cleaned. Diane would pick them up, and I would stomp them down. She didn't let me get away with this behavior. She'd immediately pick up my foot, hold it more tightly, and clean it.

There were other things she didn't allow me to do either, like tugging hard on the lead rope to get nibbles of grass. I was learning it was easier to follow her rules than resist. She seemed to have endless patience and persistence.

For the most part, I was starting to feel more comfortable around Diane. By being clear, fair, and consistent, she was proving she was worthy of my trust. I quickly earned the nickname "snuggle-bug."

I got this name because I like to snuggle my big head into the chest of people when I felt relaxed. I'd curl my neck around Diane, dropping it low so it rested against her. She'd slowly pat my neck and I'd partially close my eyes. Sometimes we stood like this for several minutes listening to each other breathe.

I also liked to pick things up with my mouth when I was feeling playful. I especially liked the orange cones in the arena. I picked them up, dropped them, then picked them up again until Diane told me it was time to move on. I also liked

Diane's water bottles. She always had one with her, and I tried to pick them up or at least put my mouth on the top of them regularly.

Sometimes she'd open the bottle and pour a little water into her hand and let me lick it. One of my favorite things to do was to carry the lead rope or the reins in my mouth. Diane didn't like this and asked me to stop but if I was feeling especially playful I would keep trying. Maybe it was these silly shenanigans that kept Diane coming back.

Diane didn't get on my back during the first couple of months we worked together. We spent our time doing groundwork. Groundwork consists of exercises humans do with horses while they stay on the ground working with the horse, using a halter and lead rope. These exercises are an important part of training horses to respect their human handler.

She made me back up, move my front legs side to side, and yield my hind quarters away from her. The same part of me that liked to snuggle led me to crowd people when I needed reassurance, but Diane didn't allow this behavior.

When we worked, she wouldn't let me get too close to her. She frequently clipped a long rope called a lunge line to my halter and asked me to walk, trot, and canter on her command. I didn't like being on the lunge line for a lot of reasons, but mostly because I didn't have control of my feet. If I let her control my feet, she was the leader, not me. I didn't like this aspect of groundwork and frequently gave her a hard time.

I didn't like to back up and often wouldn't when she asked me. Instead, I refused to move or stomped my hooves in defiance to let her know I was angry. I invaded her space and pushed her body with my head.

On the lunge line I often worked myself up into a frenzy running in circles, paying no attention to her even when she asked me to slow down or stop. Some days I bucked over and over, tossed my head, and tugged hard on the line.

One time I pulled on the rope so hard it came out of Diane's hands. I felt an immediate release of pressure on my halter. I was free! I bolted as the long rope flew out behind me.

I ran around the arena several times before Diane stepped into my path waving her arms over her head. This made me change my direction. As I turned toward the center of the arena, I realized how tired I was, so I stopped. Breathing hard, I stood there feeling proud of my display.

In spite of my behavior, Diane was never mean to me. She didn't use whips or crops on my body even though I had the habit of getting myself worked up over little things. I'd run in circles until I was exhausted. Eventually, I'd stop, huffing and puffing, my body soaked in sweat. After many of these sessions, it slowly started sinking in I didn't have to get so freaked out. After all, freaking out took a lot of energy.

CHAPTER EIGHT

Our First Ride

The day came when Diane got on my back. After grooming me, she put on a saddle pad. Saddle pads go under the saddle to keep the saddle clean and cushion the horse's back.

Next, she put on a sheepskin half pad. Half pads are designed to distribute the riders weight across the horse's back and help eliminate sensitive pressure points. My back was often sore and the half pad helped me be more comfortable when I was ridden.

Next, she put on the saddle. The saddle's function is to make riding more comfortable and secure for people. My saddle is an English saddle. English saddles are lighter weight than Western saddles. They are the saddles used in English riding disciplines such as jumping, dressage, and hunt seat.

Once the saddle was on, Diane attached the girth to the billet straps on my right side, then she brought it up to my left side. The girth comes under the horse, fastened to the first and third billet straps, and is positioned just behind the front legs. She tightened it enough so the saddle was secure but she could fit a few fingers under it to make sure it wasn't too tight.

Then came the bridle. The bridle is headgear used to control the horse's movements. Bridles usually include a bit with reins attached to it. The bit is typically metal and goes in a horse's mouth to provide the rider with more control of the horse.

Some horses don't like the bit and refuse to open their mouths, but I didn't mind it. Once the bit was in my mouth, Diane pulled the headstall over my ears, fastened the chin and nose straps, and put the reins over my head. We were ready to go!

She walked me up to the mounting block and asked me to stop. I hadn't been ridden for months, but I knew that lining up at the block meant Diane was going to get on my back. Despite being anxious, I was careful not to move as she climbed on me.

As soon as she was on me, I could feel tension similar to how Sophie felt. I wondered why Diane was afraid and started looking around. I didn't see anything scary in the arena so I stood still.

After a moment, I felt her legs give me a small squeeze. I started walking. I could feel her relax as we went along. She gave me another squeeze, this one firmer, and I started trotting. Trot, trot, trot, around and around we went.

The more we trotted the more relaxed and confident Diane became. As she relaxed, I relaxed. I knew I did a nice job because she told me "good boy" and rubbed my neck often. Her praise reassured me and made me work harder for her. I would occasionally flick an ear back to listen for her as we went along.

She gently pulled back on the reins as she sat back in the saddle, I slowed to a walk. We walked a few laps around the arena to cool down. She said "whoa" and pulled on the reins again. I stopped.

Diane swung her leg over my back and plopped down on the ground. I licked and chewed at my bit, feeling relieved the ride was over. I was tired from being out of shape and from trying hard. I got the sense Diane was relieved as well. As we strode to the barn, she lovingly looked over at me while she stroked my neck.

CHAPTER NINE

The Dentist

One day a woman came into the barn and started talking to Diane. I heard Diane use the word "dentist." They talked for a few minutes before she came into my stall. She was holding things in her hands I'd never seen before.

She moved with confidence toward me. I moved away, but she followed me until I was up against the wall of my stall. I became anxious because I didn't know her. I flared my nostrils, taking in her scent. I smelled other horses and a medicine smell. I recognized it from previous times when vets had come to see me.

She opened my mouth and ran her fingers over my teeth and gums. I think she knew I was afraid because she tried to reassure me by making those soothing sounds Diane does but I couldn't relax. She took her hands out of my mouth.

I felt them run down my side to my rump. Suddenly, I felt a sharp pinch, "OUCH!" I swung my haunches around out of her reach. As I moved away, she left my stall. I breathed a sigh of relief.

Several minutes passed and I felt relaxed, so very relaxed. I was content to stand in one place. I no longer worried about the woman. My head became heavy. The weight of it pulled it toward the ground and my eyes started to close.

I began to wobble back and forth. Even though I was half asleep I was aware she was back. I tried to raise my head and step away from her, but I felt like I was stuck in thick mud. She raised my head up and set my chin down in something cold. Whatever it was kept my head up high without any effort on my part. Next, she opened my mouth and I felt something cold that held it wide open. Normally, all of this would have scared me but for some reason I wasn't afraid, just very sleepy.

She started using a tool that made a grinding noise. "Grrrrrr, grrrrrr, grrrrrr"— on and on it went. Every now and then the noise stopped, and the dentist put her fingers in my mouth. She ran them along my teeth, then the "grrrrrr, grrrrrr, grrrrrr" started again. Finally, the noise stopped, and she lowered my head.

I felt another pinch in my rump but this one didn't hurt nearly as much as the first one. I stood in the stall, swaying back and forth as I fought to stand up, my eyes half-shut, and my mouth partially open. I was drooling and I began to snore.

After a short nap, my eyes fluttered open. I raised my head up and slowly took a couple of steps in my stall. I was starting to feel like myself again. All I could think about was going outside to be with Shadow. I let out a loud whinny to let Diane know I felt better. She came into my stall, put my halter on, and led me to the paddock.

I was so focused on getting back to the paddock, I hadn't stopped to notice my mouth didn't hurt anymore. It wasn't until dinner when I ate my grain that I noticed I could close my mouth all the way. I didn't lose one piece of my food. Wow, I thought to myself, this is great!

The dentist explained to Diane that unlike human teeth, horse teeth continue to grow throughout most of their life. The continual growth can cause the back teeth to form into sharp points that dig into the gums causing pain and preventing a horse from closing his mouth properly. This is what had happened to me. It made it painful for me to eat, and because I chewed less effectively I struggled to maintain a healthy body weight.

After that appointment, Diane made sure to have the dentist float my teeth once a year. Floating the teeth means to wear down the surface of the teeth, removing sharp points.[iii] I can't say I like it when the dentist comes, but she helps my mouth feel a whole lot better so I try to be a good boy for her.

CHAPTER TEN

Where's Diane?

Not long after the dentist came, Diane didn't come to the barn for a couple of days. I began worrying she wasn't coming back. I worried she left me like all the other humans in my life. I got more upset as each day passed and started taking my frustration out on Shadow.

Shadow wanted to play like usual but I snapped at him and chased him away. He didn't understand why I was doing this, so he kept trying to entice me to play. He made gestures with his body. He tossed his head, nipped at my face, reared up on his back legs, and ran away to encourage me. His antics usually worked, but not when I was feeling abandoned.

The next time he came near me, I lunged at him with my mouth wide open and bit hard on his butt. He scampered away, but came back for more. He didn't think I meant to bite him as hard, but I did. I wasn't in any mood to play.

As soon as he got near me again, I swung my body around, stretched out my neck, and gave him another hard bite. Shadow doesn't give up easily, so it took several of these bites for him to realize I didn't want to be bothered. For the rest of the day, he sadly gave me my space.

The next morning when the workers put us out, they separated us. They did this because they didn't want me to bite Shadow anymore. He was put in our usual paddock and they led me to a round pen. Round pens are small circular metal enclosures often used to train horses, or as a way to separate a horse from the herd.

I didn't like round pens. They made me afraid.

I was afraid for two reasons, I was alone and people had chased me with a whip in these types of pens. Now, I was even more anxious and depressed than when I was with Shadow.

I think the workers knew I wasn't happy but they kept putting me in the round pen. I whinnied to Shadow to let him know I missed him. He always whinnied back. I regretted I was mean and wished the barn hands would put me back in with my friend.

A week had passed since Shadow and I were separated. I stood in the pen looking down towards him when I heard a familiar voice say, "Hi Rudy, hey buddy." I could hardly believe my ears. I whipped my head around and there was Diane. She came back! I was so happy to see her.

I immediately walked to the gate, my eyes locked on her to show her I wanted her to come get me. Sure enough, she came over. She had a big smile on her face as she wrapped her arms around my neck and gave me a hug. I dropped my head down and I let out a sigh. As we walked to the barn, I tipped my nose toward her so I could look at her as we walked to the barn.

As it turned out, Diane didn't leave me. She was on something humans call "vacation." The staff must have told her what happened because after this incident whenever she was going away she'd look at me, say a bunch of words in a serious tone of voice, and give me a hug. I knew this meant she'd be gone for a little while but would come back.

The day after Diane came back I was put back in the paddock with Shadow. I was beyond happy. I immediately went over to him, tossed my neck, and darted away hoping he'd give chase. He did. Around and around we went, running, rearing, and throwing small bucks. What a blast! I felt so much better. Diane was back, and I was with my buddy.

CHAPTER ELEVEN

Disruption in the Herd

Shadow and I were happy together but soon enough, a new horse joined us in our paddock and that meant change. Doxie moved in with Shadow and me, causing quite a bit of disruption. When two or more horses are together, it's called a herd and within a herd there is a hierarchy. Every horse has position from highest to lowest.

In the group of Doxie, Shadow and me, we had to figure out who was number one, number two, and number three. The number one, or alpha horse, has to prove to the other horses it's the strongest and smartest horse in the group. Alpha horses are responsible for keeping the rest of the herd safe just like parents are responsible for keeping their children safe.

Horses figure out which one is stronger by making the other horses move. For example, if there is a pile of hay in the paddock, all the horses want the hay, but usually only one can have it. The horse that's successful in chasing the other horses away and keeping them away gets to have the hay. They prove they are the strongest, smartest horse.

I was the alpha horse when it was Shadow and me, but we had to decide all over again who was number one when Doxie arrived. I quickly proved I was up to the challenge. Doxie and Shadow squabbled over the number two spot, neither one of them wanting to give in to the other.

After a couple weeks, of chasing, biting and kicking each other, Doxie claimed the second position, and Shadow was number three. I usually don't share my hay but with Doxie things were different. We quickly became friends. We almost always stood next to each other. We often groomed each other and shared hay.

You might not know what horses do when they groom each other. It's common for horses who like each other to groom each other. They use their front teeth to scratch or nibble each other's withers and backs. The withers are at the base of the neck above the shoulders and back.

Doxie was great at grooming but me—not so much. My nibbles often turned into bites she didn't like. She'd let me know by flattening her ears, squealing, or moving away from me. As time went on, I got better at grooming. Doxie reprimanded me less but I still wasn't great at it.

Doxie's Mom, Allison, often let her graze freely in the early evenings when she would clean her stall. Sometimes Doxie would take it upon herself to stroll into the barn and stand in front of my stall to keep me company. This was the best.

Shadow tried to be friends with her too, but she didn't like him. Any time he got a little too close, she chased him away. I didn't like it when Shadow got close to her either. I'd tell him to get away from her by pinning my ears back, biting, or even kicking him. It's not that I didn't like Shadow, but in a herd of horses there can't be two, number two horses. When Doxie wasn't in the paddock, Shadow and I hung out and rough housed like old times. He was still a good friend of mine.

CHAPTER TWELVE

Friends Make Life Better

You know I was good friends with both Shadow and Doxie, but I've never told you how pretty Doxie is—when the sun hits her hair, it shines like copper. Both her mane and legs are black, and she has a small white star on her forehead. Allison is her owner. I like Allison almost as much as I like Doxie.

Allison, Doxie, Diane and I hung out a lot. Allison was usually with us when something new happened, like the dentist's first visit or the first time Diane and I went for a trail ride. Their confidence helped us to feel surer of ourselves. Diane and I were new to this whole horse-human partnership thing. I hadn't worked consistently with a person for years and I was Diane's first horse.

I can tell some people are afraid of me. Their body language tells me this, and I can feel their tense energy but Allison has never been afraid of me. She's my biggest fan. When Diane and I first started working together, Allison would step in to help with my groundwork. I knew she meant business when she had the lead rope. Even so, I tested her. I crowded her or wouldn't back up, but she communicated with her body in a way that told me I better listen.

Allison had been the first one to get on my back after Sophie. She usually rode me bareback in the field. I didn't mind walking and trotting, but when she asked me to canter I protested. I tossed my head, moved my body sideways, and occasionally bucked.

These behaviors didn't deter her. She knew these actions didn't mean I was a bad horse. I think she had more belief in me than I had in myself. She instinctively knew I needed a lot of reassurance. She seemed to know I was a good horse who was out of practice, so she didn't give up when I was difficult. She kept at it until I did something well and then she went wild praising me. And I mean wild!

When I went into the canter smoothly, she'd yell, "GOOOOD BOY, GOOOOD BOY, GOOOOD BOY" over and over with so much enthusiasm she made me want to try harder, and I would, just for her. She also knew when to reward me. As soon as I did what she asked, she'd give me a trot or walk break.

Eventually, I realized it was easier to canter without all the fuss. In this way, Allison worked out my "bugs" so Diane could ride me. Allison was a good leader, a person I could respect and trust. She was fair, firm, consistent, loving, supportive, and fun.

Often we all worked together in the arena. We did groundwork first, then Diane and Allison would ride me and Doxie. We began our rides with transitions. Transitions help horses build muscle and strength. We always started at a walk, then a trot, then back to walk, up to trot, and back to a walk.

After the walk-trot transitions, we moved to trot-canter transitions. These exercises took about a half an hour. We finished by walking to cool off. After the arena work, we usually went into the field for a stroll.

When Diane was away, Allison usually worked with me. She would do everything Diane did—my groundwork, transitions, and she even took me out on the trails by myself. Normally, this would make me very anxious, but Allison helped me feel safe. I still challenged her from time to time, but she showed me she was stronger and smarter by moving my feet any way she wanted.

Aside from believing in me, I could tell Allison liked me. Her favorite thing to do was to kiss me on the end my velvety nose. I liked these kisses so I stood still and soaked up her love. I was lucky to have wonderful friends in my life, including Diane.

CHAPTER THIRTEEN

Today is My Birthday!

It was April 11, my eleventh birthday. I thought it would be like every other day, but it wasn't. Diane came to the paddock and I greeted her with one eye closed. Earlier in the day I scratched my eye, now it hurt.

Diane noticed this right away and I could feel her concern as we walked to the barn. She put me on the cross ties. Soon a parade of people stood in front of me staring at my eye while they pulled on my eyelid. They cocked their head one way then the other. I sensed they were puzzled. Eventually, this stopped and our normal routine started.

Allison and Stef took Doxie and Shadow out for a ride with Diane and me. We started in the arena, interestingly, Diane didn't make me work very hard. It felt like she just wanted to hang out with me.

When we finished in the arena, we rode into the field and out to the trails. I'm sure you remember I preferred it when Doxie and Shadow were with me. We took a leisurely walk through the woods before heading back to the barn.

I was looking forward to some yummy treats when we got back, instead I was greeted by two women. They talked to Diane while they looked at my eye. Diane took me off the cross ties and walked me into my stall. They entered my stall without Diane. Feeling nervous, I held my head high and tried to move away as they approached. I felt a hand on my butt then a sharp pinch that made me flinch. The women left my stall. A few minutes passed and I started feeling sleepy.

Before I knew it, they were back, they put something in my eye, shined a bright light into it, and did something that made it hurt less. I felt a hand on my rump again and another pinch, but this time I didn't flinch. I was too groggy.

Diane and Allison stood at the door watching me while I struggled to wake up. I heard lots of words including "corneal abrasion." I guess that's what happened to my eye, and for the next seven days, my eye needed antibiotics to prevent infection. I was also given a medicine to help with the pain. It took me fifteen or twenty minutes before I started feeling like myself again.

With all this going on, I had forgotten about my treats. Diane reminded me by pulling out a bag of them. I perked up and stared at the bag intently. I nudged a little closer and flared my nostrils to get a whiff. She gave me the majority of the treats, and Doxie and Shadow got some too. They were sweet and tasted like oats and carrots. All of us loved them.

Diane told me I was a "good boy" over and over. Allison gave me more kisses on the nose than normal. I soaked up all the attention and wished it would never stop. Even though I hurt my eye and my day got off to a bad start, it ended up being a special day, and my best birthday ever!

CHAPTER FOURTEEN

Franco

With help from Allison, Diane was trying to identify and resolve any pain I had in my body. She recognized that if I was in pain, I'd buck, bolt, or become disagreeable. I was lucky she was thinking like this since people often misinterpret a horse's actions.

All too often, they assume the unwanted behaviors a horse exhibits are a result of a "bad attitude." In reality, horses often are in some form of pain. To help identify areas of potential discomfort in my body, Diane decided to have a chiropractor come see me. Chiropractors work on the spine to make sure it's properly aligned, and free of pain.

A man named Franco was my chiropractor. He had a husky build and darker skin than most humans in my life. Some of his hair is grey like the hair on the older horses in the barn. When he speaks, even if the words are familiar to me, they have a different sound.

The first time he came to visit me I was frightened. I didn't know him and after he watched me walk a short distance, he immediately started touching me. He ran his fingers down my spine. I flinched where I was sore, and I nervously shifted my body side-to-side. Next, I felt a sharp prick and then another prick. I flinched and tried to move away but I couldn't because Allison was holding my lead rope. The pinches didn't really hurt but I didn't know when the next one was coming or where it would be. This bothered me.

Franco pulled something out of his bag. Now what, I wondered? My head was high and my eyes wide with fear. I shifted my weight back and forth. Diane stood next to me and slowly stroked my neck trying to calm me down. I couldn't understand why she seemed so relaxed when I felt so afraid.

Franco held two odd looking tools up to my nose and let me sniff them. I heard him call them "mallets." After I got a good whiff, he ran the mallets down my neck and a little way down my back. There was a brief pause, then "WHACK!" The impact of the mallet hitting my spine startled me but it didn't hurt.

I jumped up and away as I pushed forward hoping to get free. Diane, Allison, and Franco tried to reassure me but it didn't work. I felt trapped and was afraid of what might happen next. Franco's fingers were on my spine again. Anticipating another whack, I shifted my body away from him. I felt the force of one mallet hitting the other mallet, "WHACK!"

I was really upset. Franco stopped to give me a pat on my neck and said, "whoa boy, whoa." At the same time, Allison offered me a carrot. I nervously took a bite as I looked out of the corner of my eye at the man. As I chewed, I felt his finger on my back again but before I could jump away, "WHACK!" This continued until he reached my tail. Each time the rubber mallet came down, I jerked my head up and strained against the lead rope.

In-between the whacks, I licked and chewed. You might not know why horses do this, and there are a lot of misconceptions. The lick and chew reflex means a horse has changed from a state of higher anxiety to a state of lower anxiety also known as a release.[iv] In this instance, when I licked and chewed after being adjusted, it meant that even though I was scared, I was feeling relief from discomfort in my body.

Diane and Allison continued to reassure me. They even gave me more carrots, hoping to take my mind off things. They said "whoa," "good boy" and "it's okay," but none of it was "okay" with me. Finally, Franco took the lead rope and brought me out of the barn.

We only went a few steps before he stopped and wrapped his arm around the back of my head, pulled down forcefully and let go. My head jerked up. I heard a "pop," and I noticed some of the pain in my neck was gone. I licked and chewed. Next, he picked up each of my legs and moved them in circles, then stretched them forward and gently to the side.

Lastly, he asked me to touch my nose to my shoulder, first to the left then the right. No problem. Before he worked on me, my neck was sore and stiff. It was hard for me to touch my shoulder with my nose. He patted me and said "good boy," handing my lead rope to Diane. She gave me more carrots, rubbed my neck, and praised me.

As we walked to the paddock, I noticed how much better my back and neck felt. As soon as she took off my halter I plopped down on the ground and began to roll side to side. It felt so good! I stood up, shook my whole body, and ambled over to see Shadow. Feeling more relaxed, I began to graze.

Even though I don't like being adjusted, I like Franco. I can tell he likes me. He is always happy to see me, and I find his voice is soothing.

He continued to see me every six weeks. Sometimes my back didn't need any work and he'd pat me and leave. Those were the best visits.

I still get a little nervous and flinch as he puts the needles in my back. I learned by listening to Franco that the "pricks" are shots of vitamin B12 to make my adjustments last longer.

After he's done adjusting me I always feel better. I often hear him telling Diane how much progress I've made. I've started to learn that when Diane tells me "it's okay," whether it's the dentist, the chiropractor, or something else new in my life, I should trust her, and not be afraid.

CHAPTER FIFTEEN

The Trail

Diane's confidence in herself and in me was growing. We made progress in our work together. I was testing her less and trusting her more. It was autumn and she decided it was time to take me on the trails.

These rides took us far from the barn and the other horses. I could not see, smell, or hear them. I didn't like being so far away from the security of the other horses. The further from the barn we went, the more on edge I became. The woods had many frightening things I didn't see near the barn or in the arena.

To help us feel more confident, Doxie and Allison, and Shadow and his owner Stef went with us on our first trail ride. Doxie was the leader and Shadow followed behind me. Being in the middle between my two best friends helped me feel calmer. I made sure I followed close to Doxie. I stretched my neck out and tried to touch her with my nose as we strolled along. Diane said "good, good boy" and patted my neck often to reassure me. It was hard to trust her encouragement when I could sense she was nervous too.

We hadn't walked very far when Allison stopped Doxie. Diane rode me up alongside so we could touch noses and sniff each other. Doxie was confident and calm. This helped me be more sure of myself.

Slowly, we made our way through the woods, following a trail that took us by stumps and rocks, through tall grass, and back into an even thicker part of the woods. There were squirrels rustling in the leaves and birds chirping. The birds

startled me when they flew out of bushes as we walked by.

Occasionally, I stepped on branches that snapped under my weight. The feeling of something giving way under my foot, combined with the "crack," caused me to flinch and take a quick step or two. When this happened, Diane said, "whoa, Rudy, whoa" as she stroked my neck.

The woods were full of unfamiliar things. Stumps and rocks made me apprehensive because I thought something might be hiding behind them. I stared at them as I looked for signs of movement. I watched Doxie carefully to see if she was afraid, but she wasn't. I wondered how she could not fret about wolves or mountain lions lurking in the shadows.

I eventually saw the field at the end of the trail. Doxie picked up her pace as she neared the end of the trail. She started trotting and jumped over a puddle with a graceful bound into the field. I copied her even though Diane asked me to walk. With a quick hop I was standing next to Doxie. I was proud of myself for doing what she did, and happy to be in the field where there were fewer scary things. I dropped my head, and took a nibble of grass. Shadow calmly strolled out of the woods behind us.

As Shadow began to graze, Allison and Diane rode Doxie and me back to the trail. Oh, no, I thought to myself, not again! I put up a protest, refusing to leave the field. Calmly but with authority, Diane asked me to follow Doxie. Reluctantly, I did. After a short distance, we turned around and headed back.

We were both asked to walk, no trotting or jumping. We did what we were asked and were back with Shadow a few minutes later. Phew! Before we headed back to the barn, we munched on some grass, a nice reward for trying so hard. We sauntered through the bright green field with the warm sun on our backs. Doxie and Allison were in the lead and Shadow and Stef rode next to me and Diane.

We were half way back when I realized Doxie wasn't in front anymore. Allison was holding Doxie back to do some trot to canter transitions before ending their ride. My body became tense and I started trotting. Diane pulled back on the reins, asking me to slow down, but I was afraid, so I trotted sideways scanning the horizon for danger, and for Doxie.

I heard Diane and Allison talking then from the corner of my eye, I saw Doxie come up next to me and pass me. I was instantly relieved. I slowed to a walk. The rest of the way back was uneventful.

We stopped in front of the barn, Diane swung her leg over me and jumped off my back. I dropped my head low as she wrapped her arms around my neck and gave me a hug. I snuggled my head into her chest and closed my eyes. Our first trail ride with our friends was over. I was safe, Diane was happy, and I was proud of myself for being brave.

CHAPTER SIXTEEN

Let's Play!

Not every day is a bad day for me, just like not every day is a bad day for you. In fact, most of my days are good. Shortly after my leg healed, Shadow and I were back to having fun.

Allison took Doxie from the paddock, giving us some time alone. Of course, Shadow wanted to play. He nipped at my neck and darted away. I was feeling energetic, and gave chase. In a matter of seconds, we were racing around.

We were excited because the barn workers turned us out in a new paddock. It was bigger and flat, perfect for a good romp. Our previous one was smaller, the ground was sloped, and it was frequently muddy. The mud made it too slippery to do much running.

We ran from one side of the paddock to the other. Occasionally we bucked, tossed our heads, or came together for a playful nip on the butt or neck. I often glanced out the corner of my eye to see if Shadow was nearby. If he was, I'd speed up to beat him to the fence. One time, I looked back and saw him on the ground. He had turned so quickly he fell. Not wanting to lose more ground, he got to his feet and ran hard to catch up.

It felt great to run, our tails and manes flying in the wind! Our antics drew the attention of the other horses. Sensing our excitement a few of them joined in the fun and began running too. A couple of the barn workers stopped doing their chores to watch us, and Diane stood in the field looking on.

On the last lap, I bucked really high, sending my rear legs flying out behind me. When they hit the ground, I launched myself forward and flattened my neck. The ground closed quickly—with every stride I could feel the frogs of my hooves hit the dirt sending the blood back to my heart.[v]

The paddock fence drew near. At the last second I threw my head up, locked both front legs, and leaned hard on my haunches. I slid to a stop only as my chest hit the gate with a loud "clank!" I looked over to see Shadow standing next to me. Our chests heaved as we strained to catch our breath. We were tired but pleased with our display. Now that was fun!

CHAPTER SEVENTEEN

A Bad Day

On a windy, cold, grey day in November Diane came to visit. I usually liked it when she worked with me but this day was different. I didn't feel like working. I was tired and out of sorts. All I wanted to do was hang out with Doxie and Shadow. I tried letting Diane know by refusing to walk out of the paddock but she swung the end of the lead rope in the air by my rump. Reluctantly, I followed her.

Diane encouraged me as I slowly walked up the hill. Why isn't she listening to me, I wondered? We entered the barn. She clipped the cross ties on my halter and began grooming me. I tried to relax. Diane was talking, and I didn't understand most of what she was saying.

All of a sudden I understood, as she asked me, "Buddy, do you want to go for a ride in the arena?" Hallelujah, I'm so happy you asked. Immediately I answered by moving my head side to side. "No, I don't want to go for a ride!"

Even though I thought I was clear, Diane tacked me up and led me into the arena. This is a good example of the miscommunication I have with people. Now, I was really in a bad mood. She walked me to block so she could get on me.

As she lifted her foot up to the stirrup, I took a step sideways away from the block. This prevented her from getting on me. She got down, said "over" re-directing my hip back toward the block. Once I was lined up again, she climbed up and as her hand reached over to the saddle and her foot approached the stirrup I moved sideways again. Around and around we went. She got down, said "over," I obliged, she got on the block, tried to get on, and I skirted away.

I could tell she was frustrated, and maybe even a little bit angry with me. I didn't want to make her mad, but I had to let her know how I felt. I got tired of stepping back toward the block only to have her try to climb on me again, and again.

The next time she said "over," I refused. Sharply, she said "OVER," but I didn't move and a second later the end of the rope whacked my hip. Startled, I reacted by taking a BIG step over. I felt my back left foot on something slippery. It was the wood on the bottom step of the block. It had rained earlier in the day, and the block was wet.

My foot slipped across the step and off the other side. So I wouldn't fall, I hopped my other hind foot up and over the step. I immediately felt pain on the inside of my left hind leg. Instinctively, I held my foot off the ground. I could feel my leg throbbing—all I wanted was to go back to the paddock. Diane instantly realized I was hurt. She bent down to look at my leg. She seemed even more unhappy. Without a word, she pulled the reins over my head and led me out of the arena.

Once we were in the barn, she started tending to the cut on my leg. Her energy was different. She didn't seem mad anymore. She seemed sad. She patted my neck and made those soothing sounds with her mouth. This made me feel a little better.

My leg got worse before it got better. The next morning it was swollen and hurt when I walked on it. I spent most of the day standing in the corner of the paddock holding my leg up so just the tip of my hoof touched the ground. Doxie stood next to me to comfort me. The next day was the same. By the third day my injury started to feel less painful.

Each day I was hurt, Diane came to the barn. She'd slowly lead me out of the paddock, patting me as we walked. When we got to the barn she'd put something cold on my leg to reduce the swelling. She was worried, and I felt bad that I had overreacted. Through Diane's efforts to take care of me, I realized how much I meant to her. Knowing she cared about me even when she couldn't ride me made me feel good.

CHAPTER EIGHTEEN

Water is Fun!

Diane squealed "no Rudy, NO!" Too late, I was lying down. The cool water felt so good on my belly. As I started to roll over, she jumped off and excitedly said, "No buddy, get up, GET UP!" She tugged on the reins to encourage me to stand. I decided to listen to her, stopped rolling and stood up. Instantly, she seemed relieved. Her relief turned to surprise when I vigorously shook myself off spraying her and her Mom with water. They laughed as they jumped back away from me.

It was the day after Christmas, and it was unusually balmy, sunny and 70 degrees! Diane and her Mom had come to visit me. Diane and I were riding in the field when she asked me to walk through a trench filled with water. I got the sense she wanted to show off my new confidence around water.

About half way through, she stopped me. I decided to have some fun. Splash, splash, splash! I pawed at the water sending droplets flying. They were amused by my antics until I bent my front legs and lowered myself into it. I don't think they understood how hot I was. The hair on horses grows thicker in response to shorter days so by December I had my full winter coat and 70 degrees felt hot.

The fact I was playing and walking in the water was a big deal, never mind lying down in it. I wasn't always keen about water. Horses have differently shaped and positioned eyes than humans, making it hard for them to gauge depth.

Puddles can look bottomless when in reality they are only a few inches deep. Since I couldn't tell how deep the water was, I didn't like walking through it. When

we came upon a puddle on the trail, I stopped in my tracks and refused to move. I snorted, blew out, backed up, or tried to go around the water. The more I resisted walking through water, the more determined Diane became to get me over my fear.

She used a technique called "approach and retreat" to help me gain confidence. She'd ride me up to a puddle until I refused to go any further, then back me up until I relaxed.

Once I was completely at ease, she'd ask me to walk forward again. With each pass we got closer to the water while I remained calm. Eventually, my feet were next to the water. We'd stand there until I dropped my head and became curious. Once I did this, Diane would ask me to take a step. Cautiously, I'd make my way through the water. The first time I did this, Diane went wild praising me. Her praise made me feel more confident.

Walking through the water once wasn't enough for her though. She wanted me to be self-assured all the time, so we practiced a lot. The lower field was a perfect training area because it had gullies that filled with water when it rained.

My first reaction when she asked me to walk into the water was to try to go around or jump over, but Diane insisted I calmly step forward into the water. Slowly, I had become more relaxed with walking through. If I resisted, we'd go back to the approach-retreat game until I moved forward without a fuss.

One day when we were practicing, not long before Diane and her Mom came to see me, I decided to get curious and paw at the water. It flew up all around me. I lowered my head to sniff it. I did this several times before she asked me to take a step. Without hesitation I walked in.

We went the whole length of the gully without stopping. Diane encouraged me every step of the way by patting my neck and excitedly saying "gooood boy." Before I knew it, we were walking out of the gully and onto dry grass. I could hardly believe I made it the whole way and wasn't afraid.

Now you see why Diane was showing her Mom my new attitude about water. I don't think she had any idea just how comfortable I had become. Relaxed enough to take a bath. I had come a long way. I now know water doesn't have to be scary. It can be fun, and if I lay in it, I can cool down when I'm hot. I was proud of myself that December day, and I think Diane and her Mom were proud of me too.

CHAPTER NINETEEN

Diane's My "Mom"

Every year I get older, it gets harder for me to remember my mother. I haven't seen her since I was just a colt. A colt is a horse under four years old. When I was taken from her at the young age of six months, I remember feeling really sad and anxious. I whinnied over and over in hopes she'd hear me and come back.

I paced in the paddock as I looked for her. I thought she would return but she never did. The people at the barn checked on me frequently because they knew I was upset. They spent more time with me for a while, but this attention quickly faded.

I wondered why I'd been taken from my Mom. Would I ever see her again? Not knowing "why" this happened made it so hard. I thought of my mother often when I was young. I was sad, lonely, and angry. Angry at the people who separated us, angry I was alone, and angry she hadn't come back to me.

After a while, I stopped wondering as much. My loneliness and anger became acceptance. I realized most horses aren't with their mothers. Humans often separate baby horses from their mothers because it helps them form a stronger bond with their human caretakers. When a young horse is taken from its mother it's called "weaning."

I never thought I would consider anyone else my "Mom," but as time went by I realized I was thinking of Diane as my "Mom." She took care of me, made sure I had food, water, special treats like alfalfa, carrots, apples and my favorite, watermelon.

If I didn't feel well, she knew it and spent more time with me until I felt better. It was hard for me to trust a human but I was beginning to realize how much Diane loved me.

Whenever she saw me in my paddock, she'd yell "Hi Rudy, hey buddy!" She usually caught me by surprise and I'd jerk my head up to make sure it was really her. I looked forward to seeing her because she is always happy to see me.

Before she takes me out of the paddock she talks softly to me, pats me, then does something not many humans do, she exchanges air with me through our noses. We stand nose to nose, she breathes out, I inhale, I breathe out, and she inhales. This is a horse ritual that shows trust and friendship. It helps me to trust her more.

As she grooms me, she moves her hands slowly and gently over my body. I can tell I have her full attention. I like this and look back over my shoulder to watch her. When she sees me doing this, she usually stops to pat my neck or give me a kiss on my nose. I often wiggle my lips or yawn in response.

Diane does many things my Mom did for me. She makes sure I'm taken care of, that I stay out of trouble, and—she loves me. I don't have my real Mom, but I feel lucky to have Diane. Do you remember me saying "I desperately hoped my life would be better when I moved to New Hampshire?" Well, my life is lots better! I can't wait to see what other adventures come my way.

Wait! Here comes Diane, I mean Mom, and she looks excited.

Grooming Tools:

Curry comb - A tool made of rubber or plastic with short "teeth" on one side. It is usually the first tool used in daily grooming. The horse is rubbed or "curried" to help loosen dirt, hair, plus stimulate the skin to produce natural oils. The curry comb is usually used in a circular motion.

Hard-bristled brush - A stiff-bristled brush used to remove dirt and hair stirred up by the curry comb, with short strokes from front to back, except at the flanks, where the hair grows in a different pattern.

Hoof pick - The most basic form of hoof care is cleaning, or "picking out the feet." A hoof pick removes mud, manure, and rocks from the sole of the hoof.

Mane brush or comb - Horses with short, pulled manes have their manes combed with a wide-toothed plastic or metal comb. Tails and long manes are brushed with either a dandy brush or a human hairbrush.

Shedding blade - A metal shedding blade with short, dull teeth removes loose winter hair. A shedding blade is also useful for removing caked-on mud. However, grooming tools with metal teeth can split and dull the horse's hair coat and may irritate the skin, so must be used with care.

Soft brush - A soft-bristled brush removes finer particles and dust, adds a shine to the coat, and is soothing to the horse. A body brush, particularly a smaller design called a face brush, can be used on the head, being careful to avoid the horse's eyes. The body brush is generally the last brush used on the horse.

Sweat scraper - Several styles of sweat scrapers exist to remove sweat after exertion or water after bathing. One is a simple curved and fluted metal or plastic wand, about 18 inches long. Another design is an arc of plastic or rubber attached to a handle, sometimes with two curved blades (one rubber, one metal or plastic) attached back to back. A third design is a flexible curved blade with teeth on one side to use as a shedding blade, and smooth on the other, for use as a sweat scraper.

Parts of the Horse:

Back - The back is where a saddle sits. It begins at the withers and extends to the loin.

Barrel - A horse's barrel is its body, which includes the ribcage and internal organs.

Cannon - The cannon can also be called the cannon bone, area between the knee or hock and fetlock joint.

Chestnuts - A small callused (thick) patch of skin generally oval shaped on the inside of each leg.

Coronet - The coronet is also known as a coronary band, a ring of soft tissue where the hoof blends into the skin of the leg.

Crest - The topline of the neck.

Croup - The area extending from the hip along the topline of the hindquarters to the top of the tail.

Dock - The very top or root of the tail. It is the living part of a horse's tail.

Elbow - The joint on the front legs at the point where the leg meets the horse's barrel.

Ergots - A small callused (thick) patch of skin generally oval shaped on the back of the horse's fetlocks.

Fetlock - A joint also called the "ankle," the first joint on a horses' leg above the hoof.

Flank - The area where the hind legs meet the barrel, behind the rib cage.

Forearm - The area of the front legs between the knee and elbow joints.

Frog - The frog's consistency and shape functions as a cushion and traction device. At varying times during the year (usually twice a year) the frog sheds. When this happens, the horse's feet are usually tender for a short time.

Gaskin - The large muscle on the hind leg above the hock and below the stifle.

Heel - The back of the horse's hoof or foot.

Hip - The area below where the loin and croup meet.

Hock - The large joint on the hind leg between the gaskin and the cannon bone.

Hoof - The hard foot of the horse that comes in contact with the ground. It is the stronger, tougher version of a human fingernail.

Knee - The large joint on the front legs above the cannon bone and below the forearm.

Loin - The loin area is right behind where the saddle sits. It extends from the last rib to the croup.

Muzzle - Includes the chin, mouth, and nostrils on the horse's face.

Pastern - Part of the leg between the coronary band and the fetlock. There are two bones which are held together by two ligaments to form the pastern joint.

Poll - On the top of the horses head, behind/between the horses ears.

Shoulder - Runs from the withers to the point of the shoulder on a horse's chest.

Stifle - Functions similar to a human knee, located on the hind leg above the gaskin.

Tail - A horse's tail is the long, thick hairs growing down from the dock.

Withers - At the top of the shoulders between the neck and back, considered the highest point on a horse.

Other Terms:

Blanket - A blanket is intended for keeping a horse warm and protected from wind or other elements.

Colic - Abdominal pain.

Dressage - This is a sport involving the execution of precise movements by a trained horse in response to barely perceptible signals from its rider. The word dressage means "training" in French. Particularly important are the animal's pace and bearing in performing walks, trots, canters, and more specialized maneuvers.

Farrier - A person who specializes in equine hoof care, including the trimming and balancing of horses' hooves and the placing of shoes on their hooves, if necessary.

Halter - Tack put on the face of the horse to control its movements from the ground. It may be confused with the bridle, typically used to control the horse when on a person is on its back. The halter is used to lead or tie up the horse.

Lead rope - A rope with a clip that attaches to the halter to lead or walk the horse.

Paddock - A small field near a stable where horses exercise.

Prey animal - An animal hunted for food by humans or other predatory animals such lions, bears, wolves, etc.

Stable blanket - A blanket typically used when the horse is inside the stable/stall. They're usually not waterproof, but many are water repellent or moisture-resistant to guard against urine or manure stains.

Tack - Equipment used on domesticated horses such as saddles, stirrups, bridles, halters, reins, bits, harnesses, martingales, and breastplates. Equipping a horse is often referred to as tacking up.

Gaits of the Horse:

Walk - The walk is a four-beat gait that averages about four miles per hour. When walking, a horse's legs follow this sequence: left hind leg, left front leg, right hind leg, right front leg, in a regular 1-2-3-4 beat. At the walk, the horse alternates between having three or two feet on the ground. A horse moves its head and neck in a slight up and down motion that helps maintain balance.

Trot - The trot is a two-beat gait that has a wide variation in possible speeds, but averages about eight miles per hour. A very slow trot is sometimes referred to as a jog.

Canter - The canter is a controlled, three-beat gait that usually is a bit faster than the average trot, but slower than the gallop. The average speed of a canter is 10–17 mph, depending on the length of the stride of the horse.

Gallop - The gallop is very much like the canter, except faster. It covers more ground, and the three-beat canter changes to a four-beat gait. It is the fastest gait of the horse, averaging about 25 to 30 miles per hour, and in the wild, animals break into a gallop to flee predators or simply cover short distances quickly. Horses seldom will gallop more than one or two miles before they need to rest, though horses can sustain a moderately paced gallop for longer distances before they become winded and have to slow down. The gallop is also the gait of the classic race horse.

Collected or rounded - Collections occur when a horse carries more weight on the hind legs than the front legs. The horse draws its body together so it becomes like a giant spring whose stored energy can be reclaimed for fighting or running from a predator.

Hollow back - Often occurs because the horse hasn't been taught to carry a rider properly. A horse that has a hollow back, or sway back, will be carrying its head up, with its back concave or 'hollowed'.

Track up - This is when the hind foot steps into the foot print that has just been made by the fore foot on the same side. Tracking up can be a useful indicator of how the horse is working.

Extension - Lengthening of the horses gait at the trot.

Lame - Lameness is an abnormal gait or stance of an animal. Lameness is a common veterinary problem in horses.

Rear - Rearing occurs when a horse "stands up" on its hind legs with the forelegs off the ground. Rearing may be linked to fright, aggression, excitement, disobedience, or pain. It is not uncommon to see stallions rearing in the wild when they fight, while striking at their opponent with their front legs.

Buck - Bucking is a movement performed by a horse when the animal lowers its head and raises its hindquarters into the air, usually while kicking out with the hind legs.

Ways Horses Communicate:

Blow - Much like a snort, the horse exhales through his nose with his mouth shut but the blow doesn't create the vibrating or fluttering noise. It's usually used when a horse is curious, or when a horse meets another horse.

Cocked hind leg - When a horse rests the leading edge of the hoof on the ground and drops his hip in combination with a lowered head or ears hanging to the side, it's a sign of a relaxed or resting horse. A cocked hind hoof can also indicate the horse is irritated or defensive and considering kicking.

Ears - Forward facing ears indicate the horse is alert, paying attention, or interested in what's in front of him. If the ears are pinned back close to the neck, the horse is angry and may be about to bite or kick. If they are turned out to the side, the horse is relaxed or asleep and isn't attuned to what's going on around him. If his ears are pointed back but not pinned back, it means he's listening to something behind him. If the horse is rapidly swiveling his ears or flicking them back and forth, this is a sign the horse is in a heightened state of alertness or anxiety.

Eyes - Soft or partially closed eyes signal the horse is relaxed or asleep. Wide eyes indicate the horse is alert and may be thinking of fleeing. If the whites of the horse's eyes are showing, this is a sign fear or anger.

Neigh (or whinny) - A sound they make with their mouth that starts out as a squeal, but ends up as a nicker. It's the loudest and longest of the sounds a horse makes. It's not a sound of fear but often is used when a horse is separated from other horses or people.

Nicker - The horse creates a vibrating sound with his mouth closed, from his vocal cords. The strength and tone of the nicker vary greatly, and will tell you what the horse is saying. For example, a nicker may be used when the horse is saying "good to see you" or "come closer."

Pawing - Usually a sign of boredom or impatience.

Raised hind leg - May indicate irritation or annoyance with a horse or person behind him and is threatening to kick.

Sigh - The horse draws in a deep breath, then lets it out slowly and audibly through its mouth or nostrils. It can express relief, boredom, or may be used to express that the horse is more relaxed.

Squeal - A horse usually squeals with its mouth closed. It can be short and quiet or loud and long. Squeals can be heard from far away if the horse squeals loud enough.

Snort - The horse usually holds his head high while exhaling through the nose with his mouth shut. The strong exhale creates a vibration or flutter sounds in the nostrils. The snort lasts about one second. The snort can be heard up to 30 feet away and may be an indication danger is nearby.

Striking - A forceful forward kick with a front leg that can be either aggressive or defensive.

Stomping - Indicates irritation usually something minor such as biting flies but he may also use it when he's frustrated with something a human is doing.

Tail (clamped) - A nervous or stressed horse will press his tail down, and may tuck his hindquarters.

Tail (raised or "flagged) - When carried above the level of the horses back it's a sign of excitement.

Tail (rapid swishing) - The horse is irritated or angry.

Tail (wringing) - Often indicates the horse is in pain.

Horse Anatomy:

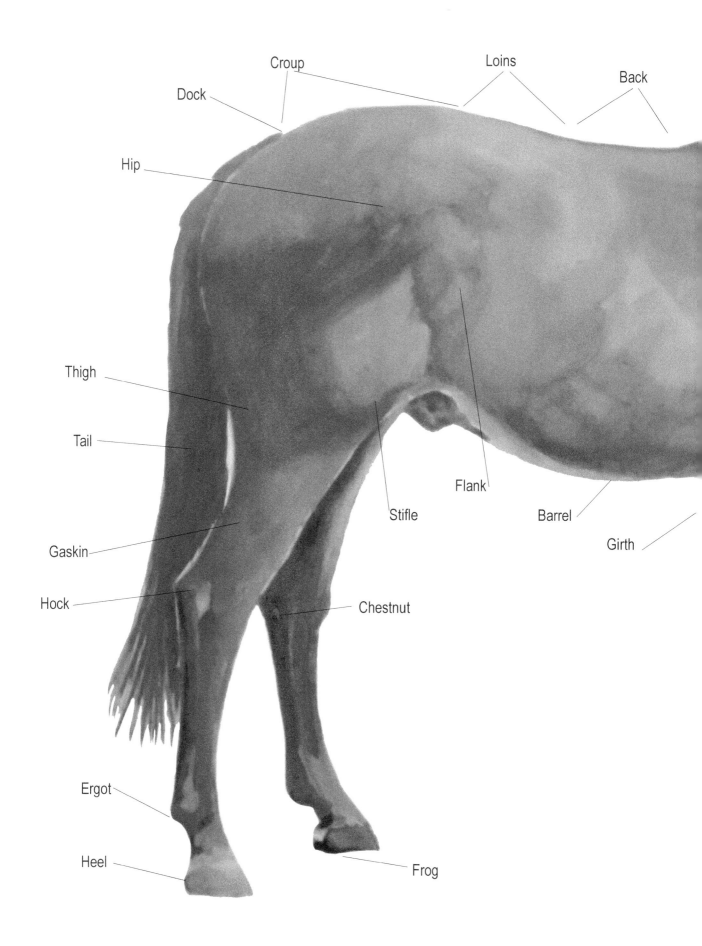

Croup

Loins

Back

Dock

Hip

Thigh

Tail

Flank

Stifle

Gaskin

Barrel

Girth

Hock

Chestnut

Ergot

Heel

Frog

Ear

Crest

Poll

Mane

Forehead

Withers

Eye

Throat

Nostrils

Chin

Shoulder

Breast

Forearm

Knee

Cannon Bone

Flexor Tendons

Fetlock

Pastern

Coronet

20 Fun Horse Facts:

1. Horses have been on earth for a long time, approximately 55 million years. To help you understand how long this is, dinosaurs lived between 230 and 65 million years ago and they've been extinct for 66 million years.

2. Horses sleep two ways, lying down and standing up.

3. Horse's eyes are on the side of their head helping them see almost 360 degrees at one time.

4. The average lifespan for a horse is 25-30 years.

5. There are over 350 different breeds of ponies and horses in the world today.

6. Horses produce approximately 10 gallons of saliva a day.

7. Horses drink at least 25 gallons of water a day and more when it's hot outside.

8. Horses with pink skin can get a sun burn.

9. You can tell if a horse is cold by feeling behind their ears. If that area is cold, so is the horse.

10. Horses are social animals and will get lonely if kept alone. They will mourn the passing of a companion.

11. Horses can be bathed by being wet down with a hose or by being sponged off with water from a bucket. Horses don't require bathing and many horses live their entire lives without a bath. However, horses are often hosed off with water after a heavy workout as part of the cooling down process, and are often given baths prior to horse shows. They must be trained to accept bathing, as a hose and running water are unfamiliar objects and initially may frighten a horse.

12. Horse hooves are similar to human's finger nails and like finger nails are trimmed to prevent them from growing too long. Horses need to have their hooves trimmed every four to six weeks.

13. The fastest recorded sprinting speed of a horse was 55 mph. Most horses gallop at around 27 mph.

14. Horses have emotions too. Horses feel simple emotions such as fear, anger, curiosity, confusion, sadness, and happiness.

15. Some horses wear shoes. Often made of metal and designed to protect the horse's hoof from wear.

16. Horses get colds and the flu. Just like people, horses can get the cold or flu resulting in a fever, runny nose, lack of appetite, mild depression, and a cough.

17. Horse's hoof growth and hair growth depend on the amount of light in the days, not temperature. When the days get shorter, the horses hooves grow slower and they grow a winter coat of hair.

18. You can tell if a horse is stressed or relaxed by the height of his head - A high head indicates an alert state, and the body may be producing certain hormones that will allow the horse to flee or fight in the event of danger. If the horses head is level or below level head this indicates the horse is calm or relaxed.

19. How is the height of a horse measured? From the top of the horses wither to the bottom of their front hoof. Once you have the measurement you need to convert the results from inches to "hands." One hand is equal to four inches.

20. When horses look like they're laughing, they're actually engaging in a special nose-enhancing technique known as "flehmen," to determine whether a smell is good or bad.

Glossary:

i Source: Dinan, Elizabeth, March 20, 2015, edinan@seacoastonline.com

ii Source: The Equinest

iii Source: Cowboyway

iv Source: kbrhorse.net

v Source: Paw Nation

Definitions:
Source: www.habitatforhorses.org

Source: www.equusmagazine.com

Source: www.thespruce.com

Horse Diagram

Source: image via www.pinstake.com

Fun Horse Facts:
Source: www.csjequine.com

Source: Cowboy Way

Source: Purely Facts

Source: ScienceKids

Source: The Equinest

Source: EquiNews

About the Author . . .

Writing served as an outlet for **Diane Robbins Jones** since she was very young. Over the years, she amassed multiple journals containing poetry, song lyrics, and hundreds of pages for a memoir she plans on releasing, "when the time is right."

Like many, Jones has a bucket list. Publishing a book has been on it for quite a while. The "universe" apparently thought she needed a nudge—enter Rudy. As she likes to say, "I didn't pick Rudy, Rudy picked me."

After working together for a year, something clicked in Jones. A story started flowing through her, begging to be shared. As she reflected on what she knew of Rudy's life, she began seeing parallels between things he'd gone through and things children go through. The two have more in common than one would think.

Jones' goals for writing Rudy – A Big Horse with a Big Heart was to have kids fall in love with Rudy, and make him relatable by sharing his emotions. At the same time, Jones wanted to educate children about horses.

Jones lives in Portsmouth, New Hampshire. She is an animal lover, and passionate about protecting the environment. She frequently enjoys her time off in northern Vermont, is an avid downhill skier, and travels extensively in both the United States and abroad.

For more information, and to continue being friends with Rudy, **follow Rudy on Facebook @ Rudy the Rudster** or **Instagram at rudy.therudster**.

About the Illustrator . . .

Karen Busch Holman, a former interior architectectural designer from NYC, is now a full time fine artist and children's book illustrator living in Barrington, NH and Lafayette, NJ. She lives with her husband, Jeff, her sons, Tyler and Todd, Buddy the dog, Patty the cat, and her horse herd of Hwin and Little Bear.

After her first children's book in 2001, *G is for Granite, A New Hampshire Alphabet* by Marie Harris, Karen found her calling. She has combined the years of experience as a fine artist, children's book illustrator, graphic designer and interior architect into one package by creating Hwin and Little Bear Press LLC, an independent publishing company.

Karen's work can also be found in numerous publications and books throughout New England. She is also the creator of the art that adorns every New Hampshire Heirloom Birth Certificate. She actively shares her love of art with elementary schools in the Northeast and New England.

For more information go to **karenbuschholman.com** and **hwinandlittlebearpress.com.**